This Morning
I Met a Whale

First published 2008 by Walker Books Ltd
87 Vauxhall Walk, London SE11 5HJ

2 4 6 8 10 9 7 5 3 1

Text © 2008 Michael Morpurgo
Illustrations © 2008 Christian Birmingham

This book has been typeset in ITC Giovanni

Printed in China

British Library Cataloguing in Publication Data:
a catalogue record for this book is available from the British Library

ISBN 978-1-4063-0646-0

www.walkerbooks.co.uk

This Morning
I Met a Whale

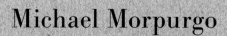

Michael Morpurgo

illustrated by

Christian Birmingham

WALKER
BOOKS

For all my grandchildren. M.M.

To Jude, with thanks also to Janet Parfitt
and Balfour Junior School C.B.

This morning I met a whale. It was just after five o'clock and I was down by the river. Sometimes, when my alarm clock works, and when I feel like it, I get up early, because I like to go bird-watching, because bird-watching is my favourite hobby. I usually go just before first light. Mum doesn't mind, just so long as I don't wake her up, just so long as I'm back for breakfast.

It's the best time. You get to hear the dawn chorus. You get to see the sunrise and the whole world waking up around you. That's when the birds come flying down to the river to feed, and I can watch them landing in the water. I love that.

5

If you're already there when they come, they hardly notice you, and then you don't bother them. Hardly anyone else is down by the river at five o'clock, sometimes no one at all, just the birds and me. The rest of London is asleep. Well, mostly anyway.

From our flat in Battersea it takes about five minutes to walk down to the river. The first bird I saw this morning was a heron. I love herons because they stand so still in the shallows. They're looking for fish, waiting to strike. When they strike they do it so fast, it's like lightning, and when they catch something they look so surprised and so pleased with themselves, as if they've never done it before. When they walk they walk in slow motion. When they take off and fly they look prehistoric, like pteradactyls almost. Herons are my best. But soon enough they all came, all the other birds, the moorhens and coots, the crested grebes and the swans,

8

the cormorants and the ducks. This morning I saw an egret too, perched on a buoy out in the river, and you don't see many of those. They're quite like herons, only much smaller, and white, snow-white. He was so beautiful. I couldn't take my eyes off him.

I was watching him through my binoculars, and he was looking right back at me. It was like he was asking me, "Hey you, what are you doing here? This is my river, don't you know?" Suddenly, without any warning, he lifted off. Then they all lifted off, all the birds on the shore, all the birds in the river. It was really strange. It was just as if I'd fired a gun or something, but I hadn't. I looked around. There wasn't a single bird anywhere. They'd all disappeared. For a while the river was completely still and empty and silent, like it was holding its breath almost, waiting for something that was about to happen. I was doing the same.

Then I spotted something slicing slowly through the water towards me. It was a fin. Shark! I thought. Shark! And a warm shiver of fear crept up my back. Then I saw the head and knew at once it couldn't be a shark. It was more like a dolphin, but it wasn't. It wasn't quite the right shape. It was too big and too long to be a dolphin. It was big enough to be a whale, a real whale. Now I knew what it was. With a face like that I knew at once that it had to be a bottle-nosed whale. It's the only whale that's got a face like a dolphin. (I know quite a lot about whales because my uncle sent me a whale poster he'd got out of a newspaper, and I've had it pinned up in my bedroom over my bed ever since. So that's why I can recognise just about all the whales in the world, narwhals, belugas, sperm whales, pilot whales, minkies, bottle-nose whales, the lot.)

To begin with I just stood there and stared. I

thought I was still dreaming. I couldn't take it in. I couldn't believe my eyes. I mean, a whale in the Thames, a whale in Battersea! He was close to the shore now, in shallower water, and still coming towards me. I could see almost all of him, from his head to his tail. But after a bit, I could see he wasn't really swimming any more, he was just lying there in the shallows, puffing and blowing a bit from time to time. He must be resting, I thought, tired out after a long journey perhaps. And then I noticed he was watching me as hard as I was watching him, almost like he was trying to stare me out, except I could tell from the gentleness in his eye that he wasn't being unfriendly towards me. He was interested in me, that's all, as interested as I was in him.

That's when I knew – don't ask me how, I just knew – that he wanted me to come closer to him.

I climbed the wall and ran along the shore. The tide was already going out fast. I could see at once that he was in great danger. If he stayed where he was he'd soon be stranded. I was walking slowly, so as not to alarm him. Then I crouched down as close as I could get to him, the water lapping all around me. His great domed head was only just out of my reach. We were practically face-to-face, eye-to-eye. He had eyes that seemed to be able to look right into me. He was seeing everything I was thinking.

I was sure he was expecting me to say something. So I did.

"What are you doing here?" I asked him. "You're a bottle-nose whale, aren't you? You shouldn't be here at all. You don't belong in the Thames. On my whale poster it says you live in the North Atlantic somewhere. So you should be up there, near

16

Iceland, near Scotland maybe, but not down here. I've seen bottle-nose whales on the telly too, on Planet Earth I think it was. There were lots of you all together. Or maybe it was pilot whales, I can't remember. But anyway, you always go around in schools, don't you, in huge family groups. I know you do. So how come you're all alone? Where's the rest of you? But maybe you're not all alone. Maybe some of your family came with you, and you got yourself a bit lost. Is that it?"

He kept staring back at me out of his big wide eye. I thought the best thing I could do was to just keep talking. I couldn't think what else to do. For a moment or two I didn't know what else to say, and anyway I suddenly felt a bit stupid talking to him. I mean, what if someone was watching me? Luckily, though, there was no one about. So instead, I looked up river, back towards Battersea Bridge, to see if any of his family might have come with him, but everywhere the river was empty and glassy and still. There was nothing there, nothing that broke the surface anyway. He was alone. He'd come alone.

And that was when it happened. The whale spoke! I'm telling you the truth, honest. The whale spoke to me. His voice was like an echoing whisper inside my head, like a talking thought. But it was him talking. It really was, I promise you. "No," he said. "My family's not with me. I'm all on my own. They came some of the way with me, and they're waiting for me back out at sea. And you're right. We usually stay close to our families – it's safer that way. But I had to do this bit alone. Grandfather said it would be best. Grandfather would have come himself, but he couldn't. So I've come instead of him. Everyone said it was far too dangerous, that there was no point, that it's too late anyway, that people won't listen, that they

18

just won't learn, no matter what. But Grandfather knew differently. He always said I should go, that time was running out, but there was still hope. I was young enough and strong enough to make the journey, he said. One of us had to come and tell you. So I came. There are some things that are so important that you just have to do them, whatever anyone says, however dangerous it might be. I believe that. And besides, I promised Grandfather before he died. I promised him I'd come and find you. And I always keep my promises. Do you keep your promises?"

I could just about manage a nod but that was all. I tried, but I couldn't speak a word. I thought maybe I was going mad, seeing things that weren't there, hearing voices that weren't real, and suddenly that really terrified me. That was why I backed away from him. I was just about ready to run off when he spoke again.

"It's all right," he said. "Don't be frightened. I want you to stay. I want you to listen to me. I've come a very long way to talk to you, and I haven't got long."

His tail thrashed suddenly, showering me with water, and that made me laugh. But then I could see it was serious. He was rolling from one side to the other, rocking himself violently. Now I saw what it was that he was struggling to do. He was trying to back himself out into deeper water, struggling to keep himself afloat. I wanted to help him, but I didn't know how. All I could do was stand there and watch from the shore. It took him a while before he was out into deeper water and able to swim free again. He was blowing hard. I could tell he'd given himself a terrible fright. He swam off into the middle of the river, and then just disappeared completely under the water.

I stood there for ages and ages, looking for him up

and down the river – he could have gone anywhere. I was longing for him to surface, longing to see him again, worried that he'd never dare risk it again. But he did, though when he came back towards me this time he kept his distance. Only his head was showing now, and just occasionally his fin. "I've got to watch it," he said. "The tide is going out all the time. Grandfather warned me about it, they all warned me. 'Stay clear of the shore', they told me. 'Once you're beached you're as good as dead.' We can breathe all right out of the water, that's not the problem. But we need water to float in. We can't survive long if we get stranded. We're big, you see, too heavy for our own good. We need water around us to survive. If we're not afloat we soon crush ourselves to death. And I don't want that to happen, do I?"

Maybe I got used to him speaking to me like this, I don't know. Or maybe I just wanted to hear more.

Either way, I just didn't feel at all scared any more. I found myself walking back along the shore to be closer to him, and crouching down again to talk to him. I had things I needed to ask him.

"But I still don't really understand," I said. "You said you'd come to talk to me, didn't you? That means you didn't get lost at all, did you?"

"No, I didn't get lost," he told me. "Whales don't get lost, well not that often anyway. We tell each other where we are all the time, what's going on all around the world. What we see we share. So each and everyone of us has a kind of map of the oceans, all the mountains and valleys under the sea, all the rivers and creeks, the coast of every continent, and every island, every rock – it's inside our heads. We grow up learning it. That's why we don't get lost." He paused for a while, puffing hard through his blowhole. Talking was exhausting for him, I could see that.

"But we do get tired," he went on, "and we get old too, and we get sick, just like people do. We've a lot more in common with people than you know. We've got this earth in common for a start – and that's why I've come all this way to see you. We don't just share it with whales, but with every living thing. With people too. I've come to help you to save yourselves before it's too late, because if you save yourselves, then you'll be saving us too. It's like Grandfather said: we can't survive without you and you can't survive without us."

I didn't have a clue what he was on about, but I didn't dare say so. But I felt his eye searching out my thoughts. "You don't really know what I'm talking about, do you?" I shook my head. "Then I think the best thing I can do is to tell you about Grandfather, because it all began with Grandfather. When I was little, Grandfather was always going off

25

on his travels, voyages of discovery, he called them. All over the world he went. We hardly ever saw him. Sometimes he was away for so long we all thought he was never coming back, and he wasn't all that good about keeping in touch either. He was a sort of adventurer, my grandfather, an explorer. He liked to go to places where no whale had ever been before.

"Then one day - it was some time ago now, when I was quite little - he came back from his travels and told us an amazing story. Ever since I first heard that story, I dreamed of going where Grandfather had gone, of seeing what he had seen. Grandfather had gone off to explore an unknown river, to follow it inland as far as he could go. No other whale had ever before dared to go there, as far as anyone knew anyway. All he knew of this river was that a couple of narwhals had been beached there in the mouth of the river a long time ago.

They never made it back out to sea. The warning had gone out all over the oceans, and that was why whales had avoided the river ever since.

"It took a while for Grandfather to find it, but when he did he just kept on swimming. On and on he swam right into the middle of the biggest city he'd ever seen. It was teeming with life. Everywhere he looked there were great cranes leaning out over the river, and towering wharfs and busy docks. Everywhere there were boats and barges. He saw cars and trains and great red buses. And at night the lights were so bright that the whole sky was bright with them. It was a magical city, a place of bridges and towers and spires. And everywhere there were people, crowds of them, more than he'd ever seen before, more than he'd ever imagined there could be. He wanted to stay longer, to explore further upstream, to discover more. It was a wonderful place,

but Grandfather knew it was dangerous too. The further upriver he swam, the shallower the waters around him were becoming. There were boats and barges everywhere, and he knew that if he wasn't very careful any one of them could run him down, and be the death of him. When a propeller took a nick out of his fin, he decided it was time to leave. And besides, he was weak with hunger by this time. He knew he couldn't go any further.

"So he turned around and tried to swim back the way he'd come, back out to sea. But that was when he found that the tide was going down fast. He was having to keep to the deep channels, but so were all the boats and the barges of course. There was danger all around him. He was so busy looking out for boats, that he didn't notice how shallow the water was getting all around him. Grandfather knew, as all whales do, just how easy it is to get yourself stranded. He always said it was his own fault that he got stranded. He lost concentration. But Grandfather got lucky. Some children saw him floundering there in the shallows, and came running down to the river to help him. They helped him back into the water, and then stayed with him till they were sure he was going to be all right. They saved his life, those children, and he never forgot it. 'When you get there, find a child,' he told me, 'because children are kind. They'll help you, they'll listen, they'll believe you.' So you see, it was only because of those children that Grandfather managed to find his way back out to the open sea again, and come back to us and tell us his story."

That was when I noticed that all the birds were back again, the egret too on his buoy out in the river. They had gathered nearby. There were pigeons and blackbirds perching on the trees behind me. On the shore not far away from me a beady-eyed heron stood stock still, and there was a family of ducks bobbing about on the river, a couple of cormorants amongst them, all looking at the whale but none of them too close. And like me, they were listening. Even the trees seemed to be listening.

The whale spoke again. "Grandfather told me exactly how to get here, just how many days south I had to swim. He said I had to look out for the fishing boats and their nets, not to hug the coast-line, because that was where there were always more boats about. He warned me about the currents and the tides, told me where the deep channels were in the river, and not to show myself till I had to. I mustn't stay too long. I mustn't swim too far up river.

I mustn't go any further than I had to. 'You'll want to,' he told me, 'just like I did. When you find a child that'll be far enough. And when you find him, tell him all I've told you, what we whales all know and people refuse to understand. Tell him it's our last chance and their last chance. And you must make sure it's a child you tell. The old ones are greedy. They have hard hearts and closed minds, or they would not have done what they have done. They're too old to listen, too old to change. The young ones will listen and understand. Just like they saved me, they can save the world. If they know, they will want to put it right – I know they will. They just need telling. All you have to do is tell them.' That's what Grandfather told me. So that's why I have found you, and that's why I have come."

That was when I saw he was drifting closer and closer to the shore again. I was just about to warn him when he must have realised the danger himself, because suddenly his tail began to thrash wildly in the shallows. The birds took off in a great flurry of panic. The whale didn't stop flailing around till he'd found his way back out into deeper waters, where he dived down and vanished altogether. This time I wasn't really that worried. I knew in my heart that he would come back, that he had much more to tell me. All the same, he was gone a long while before he appeared again, and I was so pleased to see him when at last he did.

It was the strangest thing, but when he began speaking to me again this time, I found I wasn't just hearing his words and understanding them. It was as if I could see in my mind everything he was telling me. I was seeing it all happen right there in front of my eyes. He wasn't just telling me. He was taking me round the world, round his world and showing me.

He showed me the bottom of the sea, where a coral reef lay dying and littered with rubbish. I saw a sperm whale being winched bleeding out of the sea, a leatherback turtle caught up in vast fishing nets, along with sharks and dolphins. There was an albatross too, hanging there limp and lifeless.

I saw the ice-cliffs in the Arctic falling away into the sea, and a polar bear roaming the ice, thin and hungry.

He showed me skies so full of smoke that day had become night, and below them the forests burning. An orang-utan was running for her life along a beach, clutching her infant, the hunters coming after her. I watched as they shot her down, and wrenched the screaming baby out of her arms. And then he showed me people, thousands upon thousands of them in a tented city by the sea, and a skeletal child lying alone and abandoned on the sand. She wasn't crying, because she was dead.

"Grandfather said all this killing has to stop. You are killing the sea we live in! You are killing the air we breathe. You are killing the world. Tell a child, Grandfather said. Only the children will put it right. That's why I came. That's why I found you. Will you put it right?"

"But how can I?" I cried.

"Tell them why I came. Tell them what I said. Tell them they have to change the way they live. And don't just tell them. Show them. Will you do that?"

"Yes," I cried. "I promise!"

"But do you keep your promises?" he asked.

"I'll keep this one," I told him.

"That's all I needed to hear," he said. "Time for me to go now. I don't want to get myself beached, do I? I like your town. I like your river. But I'm more at home back in my sea."

"But what if you are beached?" I asked. "What if you die?"

"I'd rather not, of course," he said. "But like I told you. I had to come. It was important, the most important thing I ever did. I promised I'd do it, didn't I? Now I've done it. The rest is up to you."

And away he swam then, blowing loudly as he passed upriver under Battersea Bridge, so that the whole river echoed with the sound of it. There was a final flourish of his tail before he dived. It was like he was waving goodbye, so I waved back. I stayed there watching for a while just in case he came up again. All around me the birds were watching too. But that was the last we saw of him.

And that's the end of my story.

Mrs Fergusson was so delighted to see Michael writing away that she let him go on long after the others had finished. That's why she let him stay in all through break-time too. She stayed in the classroom with him because she had some marking to do anyway. Every time she looked up Michael was still beavering away at his story. She'd never seen him so intent on anything, and certainly not on his writing. Until now, he'd always seemed to find writing rather difficult. She was intrigued. She was longing to ask him what he was writing about, but she didn't want to interrupt him.

Michael finished just as the bell went and everyone came rushing back into the classroom again, filling the place with noise. When they'd settled down Mrs Fergusson thought she'd try something she hadn't tried before with this class. She asked if any of them would like to read their story out loud to the rest of the class. It was the last thing Michael wanted. They wouldn't believe him. They'd laugh at him, he knew they would. So he was very relieved when Elena, who always sat next to him, put up her hand. He was quite happy to sit there and listen to another of Elena's horsey stories. Elena was mad about horses. It was all she ever wrote about or talked about, all she ever painted too. Mrs Fergusson said it was good, but a bit short, and that perhaps it might be nice if she wrote about something else besides horses once in a while. Michael was looking out of the window, thinking of his whale deep down in the sea with his family all around him. So it caught him completely by surprise when she suddenly turned to him, and said, "Well Michael, why don't you read us yours? What's it about?"

"A whale, Miss," Michael replied.

She was coming over to his table. She was picking up his book. "A whale? That sounds really interesting," she said. "Goodness gracious. You've written pages and pages, Michael. You've never written this much before, have you? Would you like to read it for us?" Michael shook his head, which didn't surprise Mrs Fergusson at all. Michael was never one to volunteer himself for anything. "Your handwriting is a bit squiggly, but I think I can read it." She leafed though the pages. "Yes, I'm sure I can. Shall I read it out for you? You don't mind, do you, Michael?" Then she spoke to the whole class. "Would you like to hear Michael's whale story, children?" And they all did, so there was nothing Michael could do to stop her.

He had to sit there and listen like everyone else. He wanted to put his hands over his ears. He didn't dare to look up. He didn't want to have to see all those mocking smiles. To begin with, Mrs Fergusson read it like she always did, in her teachery voice, as if it was just a story. Then gradually, her whole tone seemed to change, and she was reading it as if she was inside the story and down by the river, as if she was seeing it all, hearing it all, feeling it all, as if she was longing to know what was going to happen. Michael dared to look around him now. No one was laughing. No one was even smiling. The longer the story went on, the more Mrs Fergusson's voice trembled, and the more silent the class became. When she'd finished she stood there for a long while, so moved she was unable to speak. But Michael was still waiting for the first sound of laughter, dreading it. Then, all of a sudden, Elena started clapping beside him, and moments later they were all clapping, including Mrs Fergusson who was smiling at him through her tears.

"An amazing story, Michael, the best I've read in a long, long time – and certainly the best you've ever written. Quite wonderful," she said. "Only one thing I would say, Michael," she went on. "It doesn't really matter of course, but if you remember, Michael, I did tell you it had to be a true story, about something that really happened."

"It is true, Miss," Michael told her. "It all happened, just like I said. Honest."

That's when Jamie Bolshaw started sniggering and snorting. It spread all around the classroom until everyone was laughing out loud at him. It didn't stop until Mrs Fergusson shouted at everyone to be quiet.

"You do understand what 'true' means, Michael, don't you?" she said. "It means not made up. If it is true, as you say it is, then that means that right now, just down the road, there's a bottle-nose whale swimming about in the river. And it means you actually met him, that he actually talked to you."

"Yes, Miss. He did, Miss," Michael said. "And I did meet him, this morning, early. Promise. About half past five, or six. And he did talk to me. I heard his voice and it was real. I wasn't making it up. But he's not there any more, Miss, because he's gone back out to sea, like I said. It's true, all of it. I promise you, Miss. It was just like I wrote it." And when Jamie Bolshaw started tittering again, Michael felt tears coming into his eyes. Try as he did, he couldn't hold them back, nor could he hold back the flood of words. He so wanted to make them believe him.

"It's true, Miss, really true. When it was all over I ran all the way back home. Mum was already having her breakfast. She told me I was late, that

I'd better hurry or I'd be late for school. I told her why I was late. I told her all about the whale, the whole thing. She just said it was a good story, but that she didn't have time for stories just now, and would I please sit down and eat my breakfast. I said it was all true, every word of it. I crossed my heart and hoped to die. But she didn't believe me. So I gave up in the end and just ate my breakfast like she said.

"And when I got to school I didn't dare tell anyone, because I thought that if Mum didn't believe me, then no one else would. They'd just laugh at me, or call me a liar. I thought it would be best to keep quiet about it. And that's what I would have done. But you said we all had to write about something that had really happened to us. It could be funny or sad, exciting or frightening, whatever we wanted, you said, but it had to be true, really true.

'No fantasy, no science fiction, and none of your shock-horror stories, Jamie Bolshaw, none of that dripping blood stuff. I want you to write it down just as it happened, children, just as you remember it.' That's what you told us.

"And I couldn't think of anything else to write about except my whale. So that's what I wrote about. It was very long, the longest story and the most important story I've ever written. That's because I didn't want to leave anything out. I don't usually like writing stories. I'm no good at them. Can't get started, can't find a good ending. But this time it was like it was writing itself almost. All I had to do was to let it flow onto the page, down from my head, along my arm, through my fingers. Sometimes though, it was really to concentrate, because I kept thinking about my whale, hoping and hoping he was out in the open sea by

53

now, with his family again, safe again. The more I hoped it, the more I believed it, and the more I believed it the more I wanted to tell his story. That's why I stayed in all through breaktime to get it finished. It was raining anyway, so I didn't really mind."

When he'd finished there was a long silence.

"Yeah, yeah," Jamie sneered.

"That'll be quite enough of that, Jamie," Mrs Fergusson snapped, clapping her hands for silence. She could see now how upset Michael was becoming. "All right Michael, all right. We'll say no more about it for the moment. Now children, what I want is for you to illustrate the story you've just written. Like that poem poster on the wall above the bookshelf - the tiger one, over there. I read it to you last week, remember? 'Tiger, tiger, burning bright'. I told you, didn't I?

The poet illustrated it himself. And that's what I want you to do."

Through blinding tears Michael drew his bottle-nose whale, with the birds all around, the heron and the ducks and the cormorants, and the snowy white egret watching from the buoy. Then he drew himself, crouching down by the river's edge, with the sun coming up over London, all just as he'd seen it that morning. He had almost finished when, very surreptitiously, and making sure Mrs Fergusson wasn't looking, Elena slipped him a folded piece of paper. Michael opened it and read it. "Liar, liar, pants on fire." Elena was shaking her head and pointing at Jamie Bolshaw, who was making a face at him. That was the moment Michael lost it. He scrunched up the paper, got up, walked across the classroom and hurled it at Jamie's grinning face. "I'm not a liar," he screamed at him. "I'm not, I'm not!"

Mrs Fergusson put Jamie in one corner and Michael in another. They hadn't been there five minutes before Mr Jenner, the Headteacher, came in. Much to Michael's surprise and relief he didn't seem even to notice him standing there in the corner. He was pulling on his hat and coat. He was clearly going somewhere, and in an almighty hurry too. "Mrs Fergusson," he was saying. "I want your class to stop whatever it is that they're doing right now. I want them to get their coats on and assemble at once in the playground. And hurry please."

"Why? What's going on?" Mrs Fergusson asked. "Is it a fire drill?"

"No no, nothing like that. You're not going to believe this," Mr Jenner said, "but apparently there's a huge great whale in the river, right here, right now, just down the road from us. It's true. Not every day a whale comes to town, is it? It's on the telly. But we can see it for real. So I thought we'd all go and take a look. Quick as you can please, else he could be gone before we get there, and we don't want that, do we?" And then he was gone.

Everyone was gaping at Michael. For some time after Mr Jenner had left, no one said a word, not even Mrs Fergusson. But in spite of the look of utter amazement on Jamie Bolshaw's face, Michael could not for one moment enjoy his triumph. All he could think of was that his whale hadn't made it to the sea, that he must still be floundering in the river, still there, and trapped. He knew only too well what that might mean. He had to be there, now. He was out of the classroom, across the playground already full of excited children being herded into lines, and on his way down to the river before anyone could stop him.

By the time Michael arrived, there were crowds

everywhere, hundreds of them lining the river on both sides, and all along Battersea bridge too. He pushed though the crowds and hoisted himself up onto the wall so he could see over. There were police down on the shoreline keeping everyone back behind the wall. From the first moment he saw the whale Michael could see he was in serious trouble. He was wallowing helpless in the shallows, at the mercy of the tide, unwilling or unable to move.

Standing next to Michael was a building worker in a yellow hard-hat and muddy boots. He was screaming down his mobile phone. "It's huge! Humungous, I'm telling you. Looks more like a bleeding shark to me. And he's going to get himself well and truly stuck in the mud if he's not careful, and that'll be his lot. Yeah, just below Battersea Bridge. I've got my yellow hat on, you can't miss me. I'll look out for you. No, he'll still be here. He's not going anywhere, poor blighter. And don't forget to bring the camcorder, right? This won't happen again. Once in a lifetime this."

There were half a dozen people around the whale, a couple of divers amongst them, trying to encourage him back into the water, but Michael could see it was no use. Without him the whale seemed to have lost all will to live. He was trying to decide what he could do, how he could get to the whale without being stopped by the police, when he found Mr Jenner beside him and Mrs Fregusson too, both breathless.

"You shouldn't have gone running off like that, Michael," said Mrs Fergusson. "You had us worried sick."

"He needs me," Michael told her. "I've got to go to him."

"You leave it to the experts," said Mr Jenner. "Come on over with the other children now. We've got a great view where we are."

"I don't want a great view," Michael shouted. "Don't you understand? I have to save him."

Michael didn't think twice after that. He climbed over the wall and raced along the shore towards the whale, dodging the police as he went. When Mr Jenner tried to call him back, Mrs Fergusson put her hand on his arm. "Best leave him be," she told him. "It's his whale. I'll go after him."

By the time the police managed to catch up with Michael, Mrs Fergusson was there to explain everything. They took some persuading, but in the end they said they could make an exception just this once, provided she stayed with him all the time, and provided both of them wore lifejackets, and didn't interfere.

So, along with several others, Michael and Mrs Fergusson were there when the tide began to rise, and at last the whale began to float free of the mud. Michael stayed as close to his head as he could get, and talked to him all the while to reassure him. "You'll be all right now," he said. "There's lots of us here, and we all want to help you. You'll swim out of here just like your grandfather did. All you have to do is swim. You must swim. You've got your whole family waiting for you out there. Do it for them. Do it for me."

They walked knee high with the whale out into the river, one of the divers swimming alongside him the whole time. Michael could see how hard the whale was trying. He was trying all he could, but he was so weak. Then, to the rapturous cheers of everyone around the whale seemed suddenly to find strength enough to move his tail, and he managed to swim away from the shore, blowing hard as he went. They watched him turning slowly out in the middle of the river. And when everyone saw he was swimming the right way, another huge cheer went up. But Michael just wished they'd keep quiet. He sensed that all this noise must be bewildering and disorientating for him. But when the whale swam away under the bridge back towards the sea, even Michael joined in the cheering.

Like everyone else, when the whale dived down

and disappeared, Michael thought he would be all right now, that he was well and truly on his way, that he'd make it this time for sure. But for some reason, by the time the whale surfaced again, he had turned and was coming back towards them. Within no time at all he had drifted back into the shallows, and despite all they tried to do to stop him, he had beached himself again.

Mrs Fergusson tried to stop him, so did the others, but Michael broke free of them and waded as far out into the river as he could, until he was as near to him as he could get. "You've got to swim!" he cried. "You've got to. Go under the bridge and just keep going. You can do it. Don't turn around. Don't come back. Please don't come back!"

There were people and boats everywhere, bustle and ballyhoo all around, so much of it that Michael could barely hear the whale when he spoke. "I'm trying," he said. "I'm trying so hard. But I'm very tired now, and I don't seem to know where I'm going any more. I'm feeling muddled in my head, and I'm so tired. I just want to sleep. I'm afraid that maybe I stayed too long. Grandfather warned me, they all warned me." His eyes closed. He seemed almost too exhausted to say anything more. Then his eyes opened again. "You do remember everything I said?" he whispered.

"Of course I do. I'll never forget. Never."

"Then it was worth it. No matter what happens, it was worth it. Stay with me if you can. I need you with me."

So Michael did stay. He stayed all that day, and Mrs Fergusson stayed with him, long after all the other children had gone back home. By late afternoon his mother was there with them - they'd got a message to her at work. And the white egret stayed too, watching everything from his buoy.

As evening came on they tried to make Michael go home to sleep for a while.

"There's nothing more you can do here," his mother told him. "And anyway, you can watch it on the television. You can't stay here all night. You'll catch your death. We'll get a pizza on the way. What do you say?" Michael stayed crouching down where he was. He wasn't moving.

"I tell you what, Michael," Mrs Fergusson said, "I'll stay. You go home and get some rest, and then you can come back in the morning. I won't leave him, honestly I won't. And I'll phone if anything happens. How's that?"

Between them they managed to persuade him. Michael knew everything they said was true. He was tired, and he was cold, and he was hungry. So in the end he agreed, just so long as he could come back in the morning, at first light, he said.

"I won't be long," he whispered to the whale. "I'll be back soon, I promise."

Back at home in a hot bath he shivered the cold out of him, but all the while he was thinking only of his whale.

He ate his pizza watching his whale on the television. He knew he couldn't go to bed. He didn't want to sleep. He wanted only one thing, to be back down by the riverside with his whale. He begged his mother again and again to let him go, but she wouldn't let him. He had to get some sleep, she said.

There was only one thing for it. He would wait till his mother had gone to bed, then he'd get dressed and slip out of the flat. That's what he did. He ran all the way back down to the river.

All the rescue team and the divers were still there, and so was Mrs Fergusson, sitting by the wall wrapped in a blanket. And everywhere there were still dozens of onlookers. The egret was there on his buoy. And the whale was floundering near the shore, not far from where Michael had left him. But there was something else out on the river. It looked like a barge of some kind, and it hadn't been there before - Michael was sure of it. He ran over to Mrs Fergusson.

"Miss, what's that barge there for?" he asked her. "What's going on?"

"They're going to lift him, Michael," she said. "They had a meeting, and they decided it's the only way they can save him. They don't think he can do it on his own, he's too weak and too disorientated. So they're going to lift him onto that barge and carry him out to sea."

"They can't!" Michael cried. "They'll kill him if

they do. He can't live out of the water, he told me so. He's my whale. I found him. They can't, they mustn't! I won't let them!"

Michael didn't hesitate. He dashed down to the shore and waded out into the river. When he found he couldn't wade any more, he began to swim. A few short strokes and he was alongside the whale. He could hear Mrs Fergusson and the others shouting at him to come back. He paid them no attention. The whale looked at him out of his deep dark eye.

"I need you with me," he whispered.

"I know. I'm back," Michael said. "Are you listening? Can you hear me?"

"I hear you," replied the whale.

"I'm going to swim with you," Michael told him. "I'm a really good swimmer. We're going together. You just have to follow me. Can you do that?"

"I'll try," said the whale.

From the bank they all saw it, Michael and the whale swimming away side by side towards Battersea Bridge. They could hardly believe their eyes. They could see the whale was finding it hard, puffing and blowing as he went, that Michael was battling against the tide. But incredibly, they were both making some headway. By now the rescue team had sent out an inflatable to fetch Michael in. Everyone could see what was bound to happen in the end, that the tide was against them, that it was too cold, that it was impossible. Both the boy and the whale tired together. They hauled Michael out of the water, and brought him back to the shore. From there he had to watch his whale swim on bravely for a few more minutes, before he had to give up the unequal struggle. Even Michael knew now that there was nothing more he could do, that the barge was the whale's only chance of survival.

Michael was there on the shore with his mother
and Mrs Fergusson later that morning when they
hoisted the whale slowly out of the water, and
swung him out in a great sling onto the barge
that would take him out to sea. With the world
watching on television, followed by a procession
of small boats, the barge carried him along the
river, under the bridges, past Westminster and the
London Eye and St Pauls, out towards Greenwich
and the Thames Barrier and to the sea beyond.
There was a vet on hand to monitor his progress
all the way. And Michael too never left the whale's
side, not for one moment. He stayed by him, pour-
ing water over him from time to time, to keep his
skin moist, soothing him and talking to him to
reassure him, to keep his spirits up, all the while
hoping against hope that the whale would have

the strength to survive long enough to reach the open sea.

Michael didn't have to ask, he could see the vet was not optimistic. He could see his whale was failing fast. His eyes were closed now, and he had settled into a deep sleep. He was breathing, but only barely. Michael thought he did hear him breathe just one more word.

"Promise?" he said.

"I promise" Michael replied. He knew exactly what he was promising, that he would spend his whole life keeping it. And then the whale simply stopped breathing. Michael felt suddenly very alone.

The vet was examining him. After a while he looked up, wiping the tears from his face. "Why?" he asked. "I don't understand. Why did he come? That's what I'd like to know."

Ahead of them, as they came back into the

heart of London, flew a single white bird. It was
the snowy white egret that had never left the
the whole way out and the whole way back.
The whole of London seemed still
with sadness as they passed by
under Tower Bridge.

AUTHOR'S NOTE

On 20 January 2006, an eighteen-foot
(five metre) northern bottle-nosed whale was
spotted swimming up the Thames past the
Houses of Parliament. She swam up as far as
Battersea Bridge where she became stranded.
For two days rescuers battled to save the whale,
as the world looked on, hoping for the best.
But in spite of everyone's efforts the whale
died before the rescue pontoon on which
she was being transported could reach
the safety of the open sea.

Michael Morpurgo